Tomie dePaola's THE BARKER TWINS™

TRIPLE CHECKUP

written by Michelle Poploff
illustrated by Richard Kolding

based on the Barker Twins characters
created by Tomie dePaola

Grosset & Dunlap • New York

© 2004 by Tomie dePaola. All rights reserved. Published by Grosset & Dunlap,
a division of Penguin Young Readers Group, 345 Hudson Street, New York, New York 10014.
THE BARKER TWINS and GROSSET & DUNLAP are trademarks of Penguin Group (USA) Inc. Printed in the U.S.A.

Library of Congress Cataloging-in-Publication Data

Poploff, Michelle.
Triple checkup / written by Michelle Poploff ; illustrated by Richard Kolding ; based on the Barker Twins characters created by Tomie dePaola.
p. cm. — (Tomie dePaola's the Barker Twins)
Summary: The Barker children visit the pediatrician before school starts.
ISBN 0-448-43484-9 (pbk.)
[1. Physicians—Fiction. 2. Medical care—Fiction. 3. Twins—Fiction.] I. Kolding, Richard, ill. II. De Paola, Tomie. III. Title. IV. Series.
PZ7.P7758Tr 2004
[E]—dc22
2003022557

ISBN 0-448-43484-9   10 9 8 7 6 5 4 3 2 1

"Marcos, I'm taking you to see Dr. Woof today," Mama said at breakfast. "You need a checkup for preschool."

The twins, Morgie and Moffie, avoided looking at their little brother. He had never been to the doctor, not since the Barker family adopted him. Poor Marcos!

"No!" Marcos cried. "*Por favor*, please, Mama. No doctor." Then he turned to his sister and brother. "Marcos scared."

The twins weren't sure what to say.
"Dr. Woof is really nice," Morgie told Marcos. "And he speaks Spanish too. He lets you listen to your heart with the stethoscope."

"And you'll get a lollipop when you leave," Moffie said.
"I get a shot?" Marcos sounded worried.
What should they say? Morgie and Moffie hated shots too.
"Sometimes you need a shot . . . But it doesn't hurt," Moffie said.
"Well, maybe just for a teensy second." Moffie looked at Morgie.
Was that the right thing to say?

When it was time to go, Marcos still didn't look very happy. Mama helped him put on his jacket.

"I want Bunny," he said.

"Good idea," Mama told him. "Bunny will come with us."

"Hey, Marcos. Do you want us to come too?" Morgie asked.
"*Sí!* YES!" Marcos said. He was smiling now. He put Bunny in his backpack and took Morgie and Moffie by the hand.

On the way to the doctor's, Moffie said, "We can play with the blocks in the waiting room."

"Or read a story," Morgie said.
"*Bueno*—good!" Marcos said.

The waiting room in Dr. Woof's office was busy.

There was a tiny newborn puppy, a boy with his arm in a sling, and Daisy, Billy's little sister. She looked like she had been crying.

"Why you here?" Marcos asked.
"A checkup," Daisy told him in a shaky voice.
"You scared?" Marcos asked.
 Daisy nodded.
"Me too," Marcos said.

Morgie and Moffie heard what Marcos said. When they were little like their brother, they were scared of the doctor too. Morgie always cried when it was time for a shot. And Moffie hated saying "Ahhh" with that stick thing in her mouth. It always made her gag. They didn't want their little brother to be scared.

Marcos pressed his face against the tank. He made fish faces at the fish. Daisy giggled.

Then the nurse called, "Marcos Barker. The doctor will see you now."

Mama, Marcos, Bunny, Moffie, and Morgie all went into the examining room.

"Wow, what a crowd!" Dr. Woof said. "*Hola*, Marcos. So, who is the patient today—you or your bunny?"

Marcos smiled a little. "Me," he said.

First, Dr. Woof measured Marcos. Next, he weighed him.
"No hurt," Marcos told Bunny.
Then, Dr. Woof looked in Marcos's ears and checked his eyes.
"No hurt," Marcos told Bunny again.
"You're really brave, Marcos," Morgie said.

After Dr. Woof listened to Marcos's heart with his stethoscope, he let Marcos listen to Bunny's heart.

"*Sí*, yes. I hear it," Marcos said.

"Now, Marcos, open your mouth wide, *por favor*—please." Dr. Woof had the stick thing—a tongue depressor—in his hand. Moffie tried not to make a face as Dr. Woof shined a small light in Marcos's mouth and asked him to say "Ahhh."

"AHHH," Marcos said. Moffie and Morgie said "Ahhh" too, to keep Marcos company.

"Wow! You didn't gag or anything," Moffie said.

"We are just about done," Dr. Woof told Marcos. "The last thing I need to do is give you a quick shot. Then you'll be all set for preschool."

"No! No shot!" Marcos looked really scared now. "It hurt?" he asked the twins.

"Well, yes . . . it does," Morgie said. Then he added, "But it's over so fast."

Marcos's lip began to tremble.

"I know what we'll do," Moffie said. "While Dr. Woof gives you the shot, we'll all count to five in Spanish. Then it will be over."
Dr. Woof smiled. "I could use a helper like you, Moffie."

Moffie held Marcos's hand. He squeezed it tight. "Ready, steady, go," she said. "*Uno, dos, tres, cuatro, cinco,*" said all the Barkers.

"You do it?" Marcos asked Dr. Woof.
"Yes, I did. You're all done," Dr. Woof said.
"All done!" Marcos let go of Moffie's hand. "All done, Bunny."
"What a big boy!" Mama said, hugging Marcos. "I am so proud of you."

Marcos got dressed.

Dr. Woof put a big gold Super Star sticker on his shirt. Bunny got one too.

"Now, we can all go home," the twins said.

"Actually, Mrs. Barker," Dr. Woof said. "I had a cancellation. And the twins need checkups before school too. I could do it now."

"Now? As in right this very minute?" Morgie asked.
"We don't mind coming back another day. Really," Moffie said.

But Mama said, "Of course we'll do it now. We won't have to make another trip."

"Will I need a shot?" squeaked Morgie.

"Will you put that stick thing on my tongue?" Moffie asked. "I already said 'Ahhh' before. Doesn't that count?"

Dr. Woof shook his head. The twins knew there was no way out.

"You're the oldest, Moffie. You go first," Morgie said.
"Thanks a lot," Moffie said.

Then Marcos took her hand. "Moffie, I hold your hand . . .
you too, Morgie."

Mama said, "Marcos was brave for you. Now both of you be
brave for him."

So the twins were.

When they were all done, Morgie and Moffie got stickers too.

Then they each chose a lollipop—purple for Moffie, green for Morgie, and red for Marcos.

And, as soon as they got home, they all played doctor . . . Bunny too.